Every new generation of children is enthralled by the famous stories in our Well-loved Tales series. Younger ones love to have the story read to them. Older children will enjoy the exciting stories in an easy-to-read text.

Published by Ladybird Books Ltd Loughborough Leicestershire UK
Ladybird Books Inc Lewiston Maine 04240 USA

WELL-LOVED TALES

The Ugly Duckling

retold for easy reading
by LYNNE BRADBURY
illustrated by PETULA STONE

Ladybird Books

It was summer in the country. All
the hay had been stacked and the
fields of corn were yellow. Round

the edges of the fields ran deep
canals and right in the middle was
an old house.

On the banks of the canals grew tall dock-leaves. Here a duck sat on her nest. She was waiting for her ducklings to hatch. She had been waiting for a long time.

At last the eggs began to crack. One by one the ducklings poked their heads out. " Cheep, cheep ! " they said, as they saw the big outside world.

Soon all the eggs had hatched except one. This was the biggest of all the eggs.

The duck sat on her big egg a little longer, until it cracked. Out tumbled the last of her chicks. She looked at him and said, "Oh dear! You're so big and ugly."

The next day was warm and sunny.
The duck took her new family down
to the canal. She splashed into the
water. One by one the ducklings

followed her. Soon they were all
swimming beautifully, even the big,
ugly, grey one.

Next the mother took her ducklings
into the duck-yard. " Stay close to
me and watch out for the cat," she
said to them, " and remember to

bow your heads to that duck over there." This was the oldest and most important duck in the yard.

The duck-yard was very noisy. The ducklings walked close to their mother and remembered to bow their heads. The other ducks thought they were all beautiful — except for the big ugly one.

The ducklings lived in the yard but
the ugly duckling was very unhappy.
The older ducks pecked at him and
laughed. He had nowhere to go.